P9-DWI-062

The Boxcar Children Mysteries

THE SPY GAME

created by
GERTRUDE CHANDLER WARNER

Illustrated by Robert Papp

Albert Whitman & Company
Chicago, Illinois

Contents

THE SPY GAME

CHAPTER 1

An Offer to Help

"Look!" cried six-year-old Benny. "Watch is sniffing out clues."

Benny was drawing a picture of his dog, Watch.

Ten-year-old Violet looked over at her little brother's drawing. "I can see that," she said with a smile. "He's following a trail of footprints."

The real Watch was curled up nearby in the grass. He enjoyed looking for clues but he liked naps, too.

"Dogs make very good detectives," added Jessie, who was twelve. "That's a great idea for a T-shirt, Benny."

The youngest Alden held up his picture. "You really think so?"

Henry gave Benny the thumbs-up sign. "I bet your design wins first prize!" he said. At fourteen, Henry was the oldest of the four children.

It was a sunny afternoon and the Aldens—Henry, Jessie, Violet, and Benny—were sprawled out on the grass in the backyard. Their favorite mystery book series was holding a contest. The best design to go on the front of a T-shirt would win a copy of the latest Detective Club book—autographed by the authors themselves, Mila Jones and Jake Winston.

"That's a great design, too, Violet!" Jessie was admiring her sister's drawing of a girl looking through binoculars.

"Thanks, Jessie." Violet was sorting through a pile of broken crayons. "I just need a crayon to color the girl's headband."

Henry held out a purple crayon. "Is this what you're looking for?"

"How did you know?" Violet asked.

"Oh, just a hunch," Henry said. Everyone knew that purple was Violet's favorite color. She almost always wore something purple or violet.

"I'm almost done, too." Henry was adding a big *X* to mark the spot on his treasure map drawing.

Jessie looked over her own drawing. "I'm not sure what color to make my clubhouse."

"How about red?" said Benny

This made Jessie smile. "Red like our boxcar?" She thought for a minute, then picked up a red crayon. "Sounds good to me."

After their parents died, the four Alden children had run away. For a while, their home was an empty boxcar in the woods. But then their grandfather, James Alden, found them, and he brought his grandchildren to live with him in his big white house in Greenfield. And the boxcar had come along, too.

Now it had a special place in the backyard. The Aldens often used it as a clubhouse.

"I sure hope we win," said Benny.

"The Detective Club books are very popular," Violet reminded her little brother as she gathered up the crayons. "The publishing company will probably get thousands of entries."

"That's true," said Jessie. "Mila Jones and Jake Winston write great mysteries."

"Will you read another chapter tonight, Jessie?" Benny asked. The children were in the middle of *The Twisted Clue*, the latest in the Detective Club series.

"Sure, Benny," Jessie said. "We all want to know what happens next."

There was nothing the Aldens loved more than a mystery. They'd solved many of their own.

"I sure could use a cold glass of lemonade," Henry said.

"I'll second that!" Benny jumped to his feet. "Know what else would hit the spot?"

"Mrs. McGregor's chocolate chip cookies?"

Henry guessed. "It doesn't take a rocket scientist to figure that out, Benny." The youngest Alden was known for his appetite.

But Benny wasn't listening. He was already racing full-speed across the lawn, with Watch close behind.

In the kitchen they found Mrs. McGregor having a cup of tea with her good friend, Mrs. Dawson.

"Perfect timing!" Mrs. McGregor smiled at the children. "Still warm from the oven," she said, holding out a plate of cookies.

"Pull up a chair and join us," Mrs. Dawson invited them. "It's been way too long since I've seen the Aldens."

Jessie was wondering about something. "Are you still working at the Penner place, Mrs. Dawson?" She was pouring lemonade into three tall glasses and one cracked pink cup. It was Benny's favorite cup. He had found it when they were living in the boxcar.

Mrs. Dawson brushed back a wisp of silver hair. "Oh, yes. I've been a housekeeper out there for years," she said, stirring cream into her tea. "When Nate Penner died, I wasn't sure if my services would be needed anymore. But after the accident..." Her voice trailed away.

Henry lifted an eyebrow. "Accident? What happened?"

"Amanda tripped over a loose stone in the walkway," Mrs. Dawson told them. "I'm afraid she sprained her ankle."

"Who's Amanda?" Benny asked.

"Nate Penner's granddaughter," answered Mrs. Dawson. "Amanda inherited the house from her grandfather. She'd lived in Chicago but she moved back to Greenfield to live here after he died."

"Do you think Amanda will be okay?" Violet wondered.

"Oh, yes," Mrs. Dawson assured her. "But right now, she can only get around on crutches. I'll be staying on as housekeeper until she's better."

"What will you do then, Mrs. Dawson?" asked Jessie. "Will you look for another job in Greenfield?"

"That's a good question," said Mrs. Dawson. "I've always dreamed of opening my own bookstore. But...I don't know if that will ever happen. It costs a lot of money to start a business."

Mrs. McGregor was quick to agree. "It's not easy, that's for sure."

"I've managed to save a bit of money, but not nearly enough. So I will definitely be looking for another housekeeping job," Mrs. Dawson said with a sigh. "Amanda only needs me until the end of the summer."

Mrs. McGregor said, "You can always put a notice up on the job board in the grocery store."

"Actually, I'm doing that very thing today," said Mrs. Dawson. "Not for me— for Amanda. She needs somebody to remove the stones from the walkway behind the house. She doesn't want anyone else to fall and get hurt."

"Maybe we could lend a hand," volunteered Henry.

"Of course," said Jessie.

Benny and Violet nodded in agreement.

"Well, that's very kind of you to offer," said Mrs. Dawson. "But…just so you know, it's hard work."

Mrs. McGregor laughed. "If there's anything these children love, it's work."

The Aldens didn't mind at all. "We'd like to help," Violet said.

"We can come over first thing in the morning," said Henry.

Mrs. Dawson looked grateful. "Well, don't worry about packing any sandwiches," she said. "I'll make lunch for all of you and Amanda."

Mrs. McGregor poured her friend another cup of tea. "Speaking of Amanda," she said, "is she still interested in writing?"

The question seemed to catch Mrs. Dawson off guard. "What?"

"I remember her grandfather was always so proud of the awards she won at school," Mrs. McGregor said.

The Aldens were instantly curious. "Amanda won awards?" Jessie asked.

"She was a very talented writer," said Mrs. McGregor. Then, turning to her friend, she asked again, "Does Amanda still enjoy writing stories?"

As Mrs. Dawson reached for the cream, it slipped from her hand. "Oh, how clumsy of me!" She slapped a hand against her cheek.

"That's okay." Mrs. McGregor mopped up the cream with a napkin. "I'll get some more."

"No, no. I should be going anyway." Mrs. Dawson pushed back her chair. "I still have, um…errands to run." After thanking Mrs. McGregor for the tea, she dashed away.

Jessie stared after her, puzzled. She had the strangest feeling Mrs. Dawson had spilled the cream on purpose. But why?

CHAPTER 2

The Jigsaw Puzzle

"Sorry, Watch," Jessie said after breakfast the next morning. She bent down and gave their family pet a hug. "You can't go with us today. We'll be riding our bikes."

Benny scratched the little dog behind the ears. "We'll take you for a walk later," he promised. Watch looked up and barked.

A few minutes later, the Aldens were pedaling along the streets of Greenfield. After dropping their T-shirt contest entries into a mailbox, they turned onto a dirt road.

It wasn't long before they were biking past rolling hills and woods.

"Isn't it a perfect day to be out in the country?" said Violet, who was riding right beside Jessie. She breathed in the smell of wildflowers as they arrived at a white farmhouse with a big porch.

"I hope they didn't forget we were coming," Benny said.

"Mrs. Dawson would never forget about us, Benny," Jessie assured him.

No sooner had she spoken than the screen door swung open. "Hi, kids!" Mrs. Dawson said with a warm smile. "Amanda can't wait to meet you."

The Aldens followed Mrs. Dawson into the living room. A young woman was resting on the couch, flipping through the pages of a magazine. Her bandaged foot was propped up on pillows, and her blond hair was pulled back into a ponytail. Her face broke into a big smile when she noticed the Aldens.

"It's very nice to meet you," Jessie told Amanda Penner.

"It's nice to meet you, too," Amanda said. "I can't tell you how grateful I am for your help."

"No problem," said Henry. "We like to help."

Benny was staring at the crutches leaning against the couch.

Amanda grinned. "The truth is, I found them a bit tricky at first, Benny," she said. "But I get around on those crutches now like a pro."

"Cool!" Benny's eyes became wide with interest.

Violet spoke up shyly. "We were sorry to hear about your accident, Amanda."

"It's not as bad as it looks, Violet. Besides, I have Mrs. Dawson to keep everything running smoothly around here."

Just then Amanda's housekeeper came back into the room. She was carrying a tray with five glasses of apple cider on it.

"Were your ears burning, Mrs. Dawson?" Amanda asked, a twinkle in her eye. "I was just talking about you."

"I hope you weren't too hard on me." Mrs. Dawson laughed as she passed around the drinks. "Actually, I've known Amanda since she was knee-high to a grasshopper. She stayed here every summer when she was growing up."

"I have good memories of those days," Amanda said, as Mrs. Dawson returned to the kitchen. "There's a spot in Fudge Hollow— at the back of the property—where a tree fell across the creek. My grandfather and I used to sit there and dangle our feet in the water." Amanda had a faraway look in her eyes. "That tree is over a hundred years old," she added. "As old as this house is now."

"Has this house always been in your family?" Jessie asked.

Amanda nodded. "Ever since 1904," she said. "Brandon Penner built it for his bride— Dora. As a matter of fact, we still have Dora's hope chest in the attic."

Benny wrinkled his forehead. "What's a hope chest?"

Amanda explained, "In the old days, young

girls would make quilts and lace tablecloths and…well, all sorts of things. They stored everything in a chest. They were hoping they'd have a home of their own one day."

"Oh, I get it," said Benny, catching on. "That's why they call it a *hope* chest."

"Exactly," said Amanda.

Henry finished his apple cider. "Well, we should get started on that walkway."

"That's true. It's supposed to be a real scorcher by mid-afternoon." Amanda leaned heavily on the crutches as she led the children out into the hallway. She paused for a moment by the grandfather clock and nodded towards a framed photograph on the wall. "That's Dora on her wedding day," she said.

"Brandon's bride?" Jessie took a step closer. The photograph showed a pretty girl—tall and slim—in a gown of white. She had a heart-shaped face, and was wearing an orange-blossom wreath in her fair hair.

"Oh!" Violet was peering over Benny's shoulder. "She looks so…so…"

"Young?" said Amanda, finishing the thought. "Yes, Dora was only sixteen when she became Brandon's bride. As a matter of fact, she was married on her birthday."

"*Sixteen?*" Henry was shocked.

"It's not as surprising as you might think, Henry," said Amanda. "People got married much younger in the old days."

Jessie noticed something written in white ink at the bottom of the photograph. She read the words aloud: "Pandora on her wedding day, February 29, 1904."

Benny looked confused. "Pandora?"

"That was her full name," Amanda explained. "But everybody called her Dora for short. That photograph is very special," she added. "It's the only place where Dora's name appears in full."

"I like Dora better," said Benny. "Don't you, Jessie?"

Jessie didn't answer. She was still staring at the writing on the photo. Something about it seemed odd to her. But there was no time to think about it. Amanda was heading along the hall again.

Outside, Benny was the first to spot the stone path winding through the flower garden. "Is that the walkway?" he asked.

"Yes, it is, Benny," Amanda said. "And you'll find everything you need in that shed." She nodded towards the far end of the lawn. "Can you see it over there?"

Shading their eyes from the sun, the children looked over to where an old shed peeked out from behind the lilac bushes. "Where should we put the stones?" Henry asked.

"Maybe you could pile them behind the shed for now," Amanda said. "By the way, we always keep a pitcher of cold lemonade in the refrigerator. Feel free to help yourselves when you need a break."

"Sounds good," said Jessie.

"And I'm expecting you to join me for lunch," Amanda added, as she walked away. "I won't take no for an answer!"

"Don't worry," Henry called out. "Benny never says no to food." Everyone laughed.

For the next few hours, the Aldens worked hard. Jessie pried the stones free from the dirt with a spade, while Henry loaded them into the wheelbarrow. Then Violet and Benny pushed the wheelbarrow back and forth between the flower garden and the weedy jungle behind the shed. When they were almost finished, Benny saw something strange.

"What is it?" Violet asked when she found Benny staring at one of the stones.

"Something's carved into this stone," Benny said.

Henry and Jessie hurried over, too. Sure enough, the letters *G* and *S* had been carved into the bottom.

"That's odd," said Violet.

Jessie turned over another stone. "There's part of a letter carved into this one, too," she told them. "Looks like the letter *N*."

The Aldens began checking the stones they'd piled up against the shed.

"Somebody carved letters into all of them," Henry said. "There are parts of words on some of them."

"Maybe it's a secret message," said Henry. He was half-joking.

"Of course!" Violet cried. "I bet if we put the stones together, like a puzzle, they'll spell something out." She turned to her older brother. "That is what you're thinking, isn't it, Henry?"

Henry held up a hand. "I was just trying to be funny."

But Violet was excited. "Let's spread the stones on the grass," she suggested. "Maybe we can make sense of it."

"I bet it *is* a secret message!" Benny said.

So the Aldens lined the stones up on the grass—in neat little rows. For the next hour, they moved the stones from one place to another until they all fit together.

Finally, Henry let out a low whistle. "Look!" he said. "Violet was right!"

CHAPTER 3

The Game's in Play

The children stared down at the strange message carved into the stones.

"What does it say, Jessie?" Benny wanted to know. The youngest Alden was just learning to read.

Jessie read the words aloud:

The rings of time
go round and round;
a hollow hides
what must be found.

"I wonder what it means," Violet said in a hushed voice.

"And who put it there," added Jessie. She tugged a small notebook and pencil from her back pocket and wrote down the riddle

Finally, Benny spoke up. "One thing's for sure," he said. "It's a mystery."

Henry nodded. "You can say that again!"

* * * *

"Violet had a feeling the letters spelled something out," Jessie was telling Amanda over lunch. "And she was right."

"Don't forget," Benny piped up, "I spotted the letters first."

"You sure did, Benny," said Jessie. "You have a way of seeing things other people don't."

The Aldens were sitting around the picnic table in the backyard with Amanda, eating sandwiches for lunch.

"Do you know how the riddle got there, Amanda?" Violet asked.

"I think you stumbled upon the spy game," Amamda said.

The Aldens turned to Amanda in surprise.

"Did you say"—Henry paused— "the *spy* game?"

Amanda nodded. "That's exactly what I said."

The Aldens began to speak at once.

"What kind of game is that?"

"Is there really a spy?"

"How do you play it?"

"Is the stone riddle part of the game?"

"Let me explain," Amanda said, laughing. "The spy game was my grandfather's invention. You see, he always had a special gift waiting for me every summer—only I had to find it first."

"You mean your grandfather hid it somewhere?" Benny asked.

"Yes, he did," Amanda replied. "And believe me, my grandfather was a real pro at making up codes and clues. Sometimes it took me all summer to track it down."

"That sounds like fun!" said Jessie.

"It sure was," said Amanda. "Of course, Grandfather always gave me a hint about the gift." She paused for a moment and smiled.

"One summer, I tracked down a dollhouse," she went on. "The hint my grandfather gave me was: *I spy with my little eye, something made of wood.*"

"Oh!" cried Violet, who suddenly understood. "So that's why you called it the spy game."

Henry had a question. "But how can you be sure your grandfather carved the stone riddle?"

"Because of the note, Henry." Amanda reached into her pocket and pulled out a folded piece of paper. "After you showed me the riddle, I went into the house and found the message my grandfather left me in his will."

"What does it say?" Benny was so interested, he'd only eaten one bite of his sandwich.

Amanda unfolded the note. "Why don't I read it to you?"

The Aldens were all ears. They leaned closer to catch every word.

Amanda read the message aloud:

I spy with my little eye
something made of gold:
So follow the clues
both night and day;
leave no stone unturned,
the game's in play.

"'Leave no stone unturned?'" Henry repeated.

"He must have meant the stone walkway!" Jessie added.

"It does make you wonder, doesn't it?" said Amanda. "I mean, the riddle seems to be pointing right to it."

"Hidden gold!" cried Benny. "I can't believe it."

"But...hidden where?" Violet wondered aloud.

"That's a good question," said Amanda. She looked at her crutches propped up against the picnic table and sighed. "If only I could track down the clues."

"Maybe we could help," Jessie offered. "We've solved lots of mysteries."

Benny added, "We're good detectives."

Amanda seemed delighted by their offer. "You've got your work cut out for you," she warned them. "My grandfather was a real mystery buff. I think he read every mystery book in the library."

"We like mysteries, too," Benny piped up. "We've read every one of the Detective Club books."

Amanda's smile faded. "What?" She gave the children a sharp look.

"It's a mystery series," Jessie explained to Amanda. "Have you heard of Mila Jones and Jake Winston?"

"Doesn't ring a bell," Amanda said with a shrug. Then she quickly changed the subject. "Before I forget, let me pay you for today." She reached into her pocket again and pulled out a handful of dollar bills.

Henry shook his head. "We couldn't take your money."

Amanda frowned. "Now, none of that. You deserve a reward for your hard work."

"We already got a reward," Benny told her. "We found a mystery!"

Amanda hesitated, then tucked the bills back into her pocket. "Well, I'll just have to find another way of thanking you."

Benny was glancing around while everybody finished lunch. "Hey! There's a man in the yard," he said, pointing.

Sure enough, a dark-haired man in sunglasses was standing by the stone jigsaw puzzle. He was wearing a T-shirt, cut-offs, and rubber flip-flops.

"What's he doing?" Benny asked in a hushed voice.

"Oh, that's just Steve Kooner," Amanda said. "He's renting the room above the garage for the summer. We weren't expecting him for a few weeks, but he showed up last night. It was a nice surprise."

Steve Kooner suddenly looked up. He gave them a friendly wave, then hurried over.

"Steve's a friend of mine from Chicago," Amanda said, after introducing everyone. "He's taking a break from city life for a while."

"And I'll enjoy every minute of it, too,"

said Steve. "There are some things you can't get in the city." He looked around the table and smiled. "Like a picnic lunch under the Yawning Tree."

"The *what* tree?" Benny asked.

"The Yawning Tree," Amanda repeated with a grin. "That's what my grandfather called this big elm." She tilted her head back and looked up. "See that hollow in the trunk? Grandfather used to say the hollow was the tree's mouth."

Violet giggled. "It *does* look like the tree's yawning."

"By the way," Steve said, "what's that all about?" He pointed towards the stone riddle.

"It's the spy game!" Benny blurted out. "And guess what? We're going to find hidden gold for Amanda."

Steve's eyebrows shot up above his sunglasses. "Hidden gold?"

"It's a game of codes and clues," Amanda quickly explained. "My grandfather invented it."

"I hope you don't have your heart set on these kids finding gold, Amanda," Steve said. He shook his head. "Mark my words...it'll never happen."

Jessie and Henry exchanged glances. What did Steve mean?

"No, they'll *never* figure out that riddle," Steve told Amanda. Then he turned and walked away.

CHAPTER 4

Fudge Hollow

"Steve sure will be surprised when we find the hiding place," Benny said later that evening. The children were playing a board game in the kitchen with Grandfather. They'd told him everything that had happened at the Penner place.

James Alden spoke up. "Amanda's lucky that she just happened to hire top-notch detectives to remove the stones from her walkway."

"She really lucked out," said Benny.

Grandfather chuckled. "Yes, I guess she did."

Mrs. McGregor joined them at the table. "I'm surprised that Amanda hasn't put the Penner place up for sale."

"Why would she do that, Mrs. McGregor?" asked Violet, passing the popcorn to Benny. "The house has been in the Penner family since 1904."

"Brandon Penner built it for his bride." Henry pointed out. "What was her name again?"

"Dora," Jessie reminded her brother.

Grandfather had a puzzled look. "Did you say…Dora?"

Benny swallowed a mouthful of popcorn. "Well, her real name was Pandora," he said. "But everybody called her Dora for short."

"Are you sure?" Grandfather looked uncertain.

"Amanda showed us her picture, Grandfather," Jessie told him. "It was taken on her wedding day."

Grandfather seemed surprised to hear this. "Well, what do you know?" he said. "I always thought her name was Abigail. I can't recall where I heard that, though. The Penner family was rich. They paid for the Greenfield library to be built! They were very well known."

Jessie and Henry exchanged glances. James Alden knew all there was to know about the history of Greenfield. It wasn't like him to get names wrong.

"Time to call it a night," Mrs. McGregor said in the middle of a yawn.

Grandfather glanced up at the clock. "I didn't realize it was so late."

After saying good-night to Grandfather and Mrs. McGregor, the children gathered in Henry and Benny's room to talk about the spy game.

"How does the riddle go again?" Benny asked.

Jessie flipped her notebook open and read it aloud: *"The rings of time/ go round and round/ a hollow hides/ what must be found."*

"The rings of time," Henry repeated thoughtfully. "That's the tricky part."

But Violet was fairly sure she had it figured out. "A clock tells time."

"You think we should be looking for a clock?" Jessie asked in surprise.

"I'm only guessing," said Violet. "But the clues seem to fit."

Benny was quick to agree. "The hands of a clock go round and round."

This got Jessie thinking. "Isn't there a grandfather clock in Amanda's front hall?"

"That's right!" said Henry. "And what better place for a *grandfather* to hide a clue?"

"Or the gold!" Benny said excitedly.

"That's good detective work, Violet," praised Jessie.

Violet put up her hand and the others gave her high-fives. "We can check it out in the morning," she said.

* * * *

The next day, when the Aldens went back

to the Penner house, they were sure they were on the right track to finding the gold. They made a beeline for the grandfather clock and checked it out, top to bottom. But even after searching for secret hiding places, they were still no closer to solving the mystery.

"Uh-oh," Amanda said as the children came into the kitchen. "I can tell by those long faces that you struck out." She was sitting at the table going through the mail.

"I'm afraid so," said Jessie, and the others nodded.

"Listen, you wouldn't take money for your hard work yesterday," said Amanda, "so Mrs. Dawson and I came up with an idea to thank you."

Amanda's housekeeper held up a wicker basket. "How does a picnic in Fudge Hollow sound?" Mrs. Dawson asked.

"I love picnics!" Benny said.

"We all do," Violet added.

Just then, Jessie noticed something on the floor by Amanda's chair. She hurried to pick it up.

"I think you dropped this, Amanda," she said.

"Oh?" Amanda looked up from sorting the mail. "What is it, Jessie?"

"A business card, I think," Jessie said, taking a closer look. "For the Greenfield Modeling Agency."

Amanda suddenly snatched the card from Jessie's hand. "That's nothing important," she said, tearing the card into little pieces. "People keep giving me their business cards whenever I go into town."

Mrs. Dawson handed the Aldens the picnic basket. "Just go out the back gate," she told them, "then follow the path across the fields. It'll take you right to Fudge Hollow."

"Don't worry," Henry said, as they walked out the door. "We won't get lost."

Outside, Jessie turned to the others. "Did Amanda seem like she was acting a little strange to you?"

"What do you mean, Jessie?" asked Violet.

"She dropped a business card," Jessie explained, "and when I handed it to her, she ripped it into little pieces."

"She said she just gets too many of them," Henry reminded her. "I'm sure that's all it is."

"You're probably right," said Jessie. Still, she couldn't help thinking it seemed a bit odd.

The children were soon walking single file along a path that led through fields of buttercups and daisies. They hadn't gone very far before Jessie suddenly stopped in her tracks.

"What is it?" Henry asked, almost bumping into her.

Jessie swirled around on her heel. "We're going to Fudge *Hollow*!" she almost shouted. She was staring wide-eyed at her sister and brothers.

"We know that, Jessie," Benny reminded her. "It's just up ahead."

"It's not that, Benny," Jessie said.

"What, then?"

Jessie began to recite the stone riddle, and the others soon joined in. "*The rings of time/ go round and round/ a hollow hides/ what must be found.*" They all knew it by heart.

Henry smacked his forehead with the palm of his hand. "Why didn't I think of that?" he said, suddenly catching on. "I bet the last part of the riddle leads to Fudge Hollow."

"I think it's likely," said Jessie.

"Yippee!" Benny raised both arms in the air as he let out a cheer. "Now we're getting somewhere."

"Don't go saying 'yippee' just yet, Benny," Violet warned him. "We might—"

Before she had a chance to finish her sentence, the youngest Alden was off running.

CHAPTER 5

The Rings of Time

For the next few hours, the Aldens weaved their way through the trees, trudged through brush, and climbed over rocks. They weren't sure what kind of clue they were looking for, but they kept an eye out for anything unusual. When they came to a creek, Benny pointed to a fallen tree that made a perfect bridge across the water.

"I bet that's the spot Amanda was talking about," he said.

Violet looked over. "You mean, where

she'd sit with her grandfather?"

Benny nodded. "And they'd dangle their feet in the water."

"That doesn't sound like a bad idea," said Henry. "Why don't we have our picnic right here?"

With that, the children pulled off their socks and shoes, then made their way to the middle of the log. As they sat side by side, Jessie passed out the sandwiches, while Henry opened the thermos and poured the lemon-ade.

"We've been all over Fudge Hollow," Benny said, as he dipped his toes into the cool water. "What's next?"

"I haven't the slightest idea," Jessie admitted.

"Maybe we missed something," said Violet. She tore a piece of crust from her bread and tossed it in the water for the ducks.

"Maybe," said Henry. But he didn't sound as if he believed it.

Nobody said anything for a while. They were each thinking the same thing. Had Steve been right? Was this a mystery they couldn't solve? Finally, Benny spoke up.

"I wonder how Amanda knew," he said thoughtfully.

Jessie looked over at him. "Knew what, Benny?"

"That this tree was over a hundred years old," said Benny.

Henry had an answer. "Amanda probably counted the tree rings."

"Tree rings?" Violet gave her older brother a puzzled look.

"I read somewhere—in school, maybe—that there's a ring around the trunk for every year a tree's been alive," said Henry. "I'll show you."

He scrambled off the log with Benny close behind, then pointed to the bottom of the fallen tree where it had been cut down long ago.

Violet hurried over to take a look for herself. So did Jessie.

"See how the rings go round and round?" Henry said. "If you count each ring, you can figure out how much time—" He suddenly drew in his breath, surprised by his own words.

"What's wrong, Henry?" Benny asked.

"That's...that's it!" Henry cried. "'The rings of time.'"

Violet's eyes widened. "Then the riddle must mean—"

"A tree!" finished Henry. "We should be looking for a tree in Fudge Hollow!"

Jessie couldn't help laughing. "Finding the right tree around here is like looking for a needle in a haystack."

Just then, the children whirled around when they heard a familiar voice. It was coming from the path behind the trees.

"Of course I know what a treasure I'll be getting," the voice was saying. It was Steve Kooner. He was talking on a cell phone.

The Aldens didn't mean to eavesdrop. But from where they were standing, they couldn't help overhearing bits and pieces of the conversation.

"No, no, no!" Steve was saying on the

phone. "I have to find the ring first."

"Did you hear that?" Benny whispered.

Jessie nodded. None of them liked the sound of this.

"What?" Steve went on. "Of course, I know there's a deadline...Don't worry...I'm telling you, we have it all plotted out."

As Steve's voice faded away, the children looked at each other in disbelief.

"Can you believe that?" Violet said, keeping her voice low. "Steve must be looking for the rings of time, too."

Benny looked around to make sure no one could hear him. Then he whispered, "He's supposed to be Amanda's friend!"

Jessie frowned. "Well, he's not much of a friend if he's trying to steal her gold."

"Oh, Jessie!" Violet's eyes widened. "You don't really think that's true, do you?"

Jessie frowned. "I don't know what to think. But that would explain why Steve was trying to stop us from solving the mystery."

"He's afraid we'll beat him to the gold,"

guessed Benny. "Do you think we should warn Amanda?"

"Maybe we shouldn't be too hasty," said Henry. "Amanda would never believe her friend was a thief—not unless we had evidence."

Everyone agreed Henry had a point. It was one thing to suspect someone; it was another thing to have proof.

"Let's just keep a close eye on him for now," Henry went on. "If Steve is up to no good, we'll have to— "

"Solve the mystery," Benny cut in. "And fast!"

CHAPTER 6

The Yawning Tree

That evening, Jessie read the last chapter of *The Twisted Clue* aloud. When she was finished, Henry, Violet, and Benny clapped their hands.

"I liked the surprise twist at the end," Henry said. "I didn't see it coming."

"Me, either," said Violet. "Mila Jones and Jake Winston write cool mysteries."

The Aldens had gathered in the room Jessie and Violet shared. Even Watch was curled up on the end of the bed.

"What's the next book coming out, Jessie?" Benny wanted to know.

Jessie, who was sitting on the edge of the bed, flipped to the back of the book. She read aloud: "'Partners in crime Mila Jones and Jake Winston have put together another great plot sure to leave you on the edge of your seats! Don't miss THE JIGSAW-PUZZLE MYSTERY, coming out soon!'"

The children looked at each other in surprise. Then they burst into laughter.

"Can you believe that?" said Jessie. "The next book is about a jigsaw puzzle!"

"And we just found a stone jigsaw puzzle!" Benny's eyes were huge.

"How funny is that?" said Violet, who was sitting on the window seat.

"I'll tell you what would be funny," said Henry. "If the next Detective Club mystery has a clue in it about the rings of time."

"Oooh!" Violet shivered a little. "Now, that *would* be weird."

"It sure would," Benny said in the middle of a yawn.

Jessie had to bite her lip to keep from laughing. "Benny, you look just like the Yawning Tree."

"Oh my gosh!" Violet put a hand over her mouth in surprise. "I think we got it wrong."

"What do you mean, Violet?" Jessie asked.

"When you mentioned the Yawning Tree, it suddenly hit me," she said. "We were looking for a tree in a *hollow*. But I think we should be looking for a hollow in a *tree*!" She sounded excited.

"You think something's hidden in the hollow of the Yawning Tree?" Henry asked.

Violet shrugged. "It's worth checking out, don't you think?"

After a moment's thought, Jessie said, "I think we might be getting warmer."

"Let's just hope Steve doesn't get there first," said Benny.

* * * *

"I can't quite reach it," said Henry, who was standing on his tiptoes. The Aldens were standing under the Yawning Tree the next morning. Henry was straining to reach the hollow in the trunk.

"You can do it, Henry!" Benny was hopping up and down with excitement. "Just a little higher."

"It's no use," Henry said, turning around to face his brother and sister. "I'm not tall enough."

But Jessie had a solution. Lacing her fingers with Violet's, they gave their older brother a step up. Henry managed to reach a hand into the hollow and patted around inside.

"Hurry, Henry," Violet urged, straining under his weight.

"Anything there?" Jessie wanted to know.

Even Benny had stopped bouncing. He was holding his breath.

"I don't think so, but... *wait*!" Henry cried.

"What is it?" asked Jessie.

When Henry stepped down, he was holding a tin box, no bigger than the palm of his hand.

"Open it, okay?" Benny urged, as they sat down at the picnic table.

Henry lifted the lid from the box. Inside, they found a piece of paper folded to the size of a postage stamp.

"I wonder if it's another riddle," Violet said, her voice scarcely above a whisper.

"There's only one way to know for sure," said Henry.

He unfolded the paper, then read the words in black ink aloud:

A gown of white
young Dora wore
on her birthday
number four.

"Hey, it's a riddle about Dora!" Benny cried out in surprise.

Henry nodded. "When she was four years old."

"It's not much to go on," said Jessie.

Benny jumped to his feet. "Let's show it to Amanda," he said. "She might know what it means."

But Jessie didn't look too sure. "Maybe we

should keep this to ourselves for now."

Henry thought about this, then nodded. "You're right, Jessie. Amanda might tell Steve about it."

"I forgot about that." Benny sat down again. "She doesn't know he's up to no good."

"We can't be sure what Steve was talking about on the phone," Violet pointed out.

"That's true, Violet," Jessie said. "But I still think we should try to figure a few things out on our own first."

"If you ask me," said Henry, "we should be looking for a picture of Dora."

Benny agreed. "On her birthday number four."

"There must be a family album some-where," Violet said. "I'm sure Amanda won't mind if we browse through it."

"Let's ask her!" cried Benny.

The children found Amanda working at her computer in the den. She swiveled around in her chair as they came into the room.

"Hi, kids," she said, flashing a smile. "Any luck with the spy game?"

Jessie didn't want to lie, but she also knew it was best not to mention the mystery just yet. "We're still working on it," she said truthfully.

"Oh." Amanda looked disappointed.

Henry said, "We were just wondering if we could take a look through your family album."

"The family album?" Amanda gave them a questioning look. "There's one in the living room," she told them. "And there might be some family photos in Dora's old hope chest."

Before Amanda had a chance to ask any questions, Steve poked his head into the room. When she motioned for him to come in, he opened the door wider.

"I was out for a walk," he said to Amanda. "I remembered how much you like daisies." He pulled a bouquet out from behind his back.

"How sweet!" Amanda smiled as she reached out for the flowers.

Jessie couldn't help noticing Steve blush

a little. She wondered if he had a crush on Amanda. But why would he want to steal from somebody he liked?

Steve looked over at the Aldens. "Found any gold yet?" he asked, a teasing twinkle in his eye.

Benny blurted out, "Well, we did find—" Henry poked him. Then Benny remembered they were not supposed to talk about the mystery.

Steve was instantly curious. "You found something?"

"The stone riddle," Jessie said, after some quick thinking.

"Oh, that," said Steve. "Yes, it's a tough one to figure out. I bet you're going around in circles."

Violet spoke up. "Can we put the daisies in water for you, Amanda?" she asked, trying to change the subject.

"Thank you, Violet." Amanda held the bouquet out to her. "I think you'll find a vase in the bottom of the dining-room cabinet." As the children headed for the door, she added, "Oh, I was wondering about tomorrow night. Why don't you just stay over? It would give you a break from all that biking back and forth."

"That would be wonderful," said Jessie, and the others nodded. "We'll have to check with Grandfather. But I'm sure he won't mind."

Amanda seemed pleased to hear this. "Steve's giving me a lift into town tomorrow to run some errands. But Mrs. Dawson will be here," she said. "And don't forget your swimsuits," she added. "If it gets hot, you can cool off in the creek."

The children agreed that it sounded like fun. Then Henry and Violet headed to the living room to find the Penner family album while Jessie and Benny went to look for a vase. In the corner of the dining room was a cabinet with glass doors. As Jessie reached a vase from the bottom shelf, Benny tapped her on the shoulder.

"What is it, Benny?"

"Look," he said, pointing through the glass doors.

There, on one of the cabinet shelves, was a set of Detective Club books. "Oh!" Jessie said. Her mouth dropped open in surprise.

Benny stood with his hands on his hips. "Amanda told us she'd never heard of the Detective Club books," he said.

"She said they 'didn't ring a bell.'" Jessie recalled.

"Why would she lie to us?" Benny asked.

Jessie pulled out a book and opened it to the first page. The inscription read: THIS BOOK IS THE PROPERTY OF AMANDA PENNER. There was no doubt about it. Amanda really *did* lie to them. But why?

Henry and Violet came in and saw the books, too.

"Maybe she just forgot she owns them," Henry said.

But Jessie wasn't convinced. "Remember when I mentioned the Detective Club authors—Mila Jones and Jake Winston? Amanda changed the subject as fast as she could. Did you notice?"

The others nodded. They'd noticed, too.

"But why would she pretend she'd never heard of the Detective Club books?" Violet wondered. "That's the part I don't understand."

"It does seem odd," Henry said. "But I think we should concentrate on one mystery at a time."

The others agreed. "Let's find that picture of Dora!" said Benny.

CHAPTER 7

Pandora's Box

As they sat on the living-room couch, the Aldens turned the pages of the Penner family album. They found a photograph of Brandon Penner standing on the front porch. He had a mustache, and his dark hair was parted in the middle. But they didn't find any photos of Dora.

"That's funny," Violet said, pointing to an empty space where a photograph used to be. "A picture's missing."

Benny's eyes widened in alarm. "I wonder

if Steve stole it. I bet he did!"

"Oh, Benny!" Jessie exclaimed. "Why would Steve steal one of Amanda's photos?"

"Maybe it was a picture of Dora," Benny guessed, "on her birthday number four."

The others had to admit this was possible. After all, they hadn't found any other photos of Dora.

"We can't be sure it's Dora's picture that's missing," Violet said, as she put the album away. "I think we should look in her hope chest."

With that, the four children made their way up the carpeted stairs. At the end of the hall, they found a second flight of stairs. They soon found themselves in a dusty attic with a sloping ceiling. It was full of boxes, old furniture, stacks of magazines, and broken toys.

"Dora's hope chest must be up here somewhere," Violet said, glancing around.

Benny was the first to spot a wooden chest tucked away behind a rocking horse. Taped to the chest was a tag that read: *Dora's Hope Chest.*

"This is definitely it," Henry said. As he lifted the lid, the smell of mothballs filled the air.

The children set to work searching the chest. They found clothes yellowed with age, packets of letters tied with ribbons, and an old game of checkers. But not a single photo.

"Well, that didn't pan out," Jessie said as they headed downstairs again.

"You mean, it didn't Pan*dora* out," Henry joked. They all laughed.

Once again, the children stopped in the hallway to look at Dora's picture. "There must be another photograph of her around here somewhere," said Jessie.

Benny shook his head. "Steve stole it, remember?" He was sure of it.

"Benny!" Violet exclaimed. "We shouldn't suspect people until we're certain it was actually stolen."

"Dora's wearing a gown of white in this photo," Henry said thoughtfully, "but—"

"It isn't her birthday number four," finished Benny.

Jessie was staring hard at the photograph on the wall.

"Thinking about something, Jessie?" Violet asked.

Jessie nodded her head slowly. "I knew there was something odd about this," she said. "I just didn't realize what it was—until now."

"What are you saying, Jessie?" Henry asked her.

"Somebody made a mistake," Jessie said. "Did you notice?"

"What kind of mistake?" Benny said, his eyebrows furrowed.

"Listen to this." Jessie read the words on the bottom of the photo aloud. "'Pandora on her wedding day, February 29, 1904.'"

What's wrong with that, Jessie?" Violet wondered. "It's just the date of Pandora's wedding."

"February 29," Jessie repeated. "Doesn't that seem a bit odd to you?"

Henry looked puzzled, but only for a moment. "Oh, now that you mention it..."

"The date's wrong!" Violet cried at the

same time. "February only has twenty-eight days. Not twenty-nine. I guess somebody goofed."

"Not if 1904 was a leap year," said Henry.

"A leap year?" Benny asked.

"Every four years, February has twenty-*nine* days in it," Henry explained. "It's called a leap year when that happens."

"Then...1904 was a leap year?" Violet asked.

Henry nodded. "I think it's possible. We can look it up."

"Well, that's one mystery solved," said Violet. Then she let out a sigh. "Too bad the spy game wasn't as easy to figure out."

Benny looked at his brother and sisters. "What do we do now?"

"Chores," answered Henry. "We promised Mrs. McGregor, remember?"

The four Aldens were eager to work on the mystery, but they didn't want to break a promise. As they rode their bikes home, Benny looked over at Jessie.

"We *will* find the gold," he said. "Won't we?"

"Yes, I'm sure we will." Jessie sounded positive. Inside, though, she wasn't sure they'd ever figure out the spy game.

* * * *

"Dora wasn't very lucky," Benny said as they pulled weeds from their vegetable garden.

Henry, who was turning over the dirt with a hoe, looked up. "What makes you say that, Benny?"

"Well, she kind of got robbed," Benny said.

"I think I know what Benny means," Violet added. "Dora only had a birthday once every four years, so—"

"She lost out on birthday presents!" Benny broke in, making everyone laugh.

"Wait a minute," said Jessie. "If a leap year only comes once every four years, then how many birthdays did she have by the time she was sixteen?"

Violet began to figure it out. "Well, Dora had a birthday when she turned four...

a birthday when she turned eight, a birthday when she turned twelve, and a birthday when she turned sixteen." She held up four fingers.

"That means," Henry said, "when Dora got married, it was only her birthday number four!"

Violet could hardly believe it. "So the photograph we were looking for was— "

"Hanging in Amanda's front hall," Henry finished.

"And Dora is wearing a gown of white in the picture—" Benny said.

"Then the next clue must be somewhere in the photograph," Henry concluded.

"But where?" Jessie was having second thoughts. "It's just a picture of Dora in her wedding dress."

"There must be something special about it," argued Violet.

"There *is* something," said Henry. "It's the only place where Dora's name is written in full—Pandora."

Jessie nodded. "I'd forgotten about that."

"You think 'Pandora' is a clue?" Benny

wanted to know.

"I'm not sure," said Jessie. "But I remember reading a story once about a Pandora. It was called 'Pandora's Box.'"

"What kind of story?" Violet asked.

"Well, Pandora gets a box on her wedding day," Jessie began, "that she isn't supposed to open. Only, her curiosity gets the better of her."

Benny's eyes were big. "And she opens the box?"

Jessie was thinking hard. "She does open it, but...I can't remember what happens next."

"Maybe we should find out what happens next," Violet suggested. "It might be a clue. We can go to the library in the morning."

"That's a great idea," said Henry.

"I just hope we're on the right track this time," Benny said with a sigh.

"We *all* hope that, Benny," said Jessie.

CHAPTER 8

Don't I Know You?

The next morning, the four Alden children made their way to the Greenfield Public Library. After propping their bikes against a tree, they hurried up the steps. Jessie suddenly stopped with a hand on the doorknob.

"What is it, Jessie?" Violet asked.

Jessie nodded towards a bronze plaque above the door. "I never really noticed the words on that plaque before."

"What does it say, Jessie?" Benny asked.

Jessie read the words aloud. "'The Greenfield Public Library is dedicated to Abigail Penner.'"

Henry frowned. "That's weird."

"What's weird about that, Henry?" asked Benny. "The Penner family gave the town money to build the library. At least, that's what Grandfather told us last night."

"Grandfather said something else, too," Henry added in a puzzled voice. "He thought Brandon Penner had married somebody named Abigail. Remember?"

"I guess Grandfather got it wrong," said Violet, as they stepped inside the library. "Maybe Abigail was Brandon's sister." With that, they made their way to a long table with a row of computers on it.

"Let's look up 'Pandora,'" Henry said.

"Good idea," said Jessie.

It wasn't long before the children found five books. As they made their way to an empty table, Jessie looked over her shoulder uneasily.

"What is it, Jessie?" Henry whispered. He

could see that something was troubling her.

"I'm not sure," Jessie said, keeping her voice low. "I just have the strangest feeling we're being watched."

Henry took a quick glance around the room. "I don't see anyone suspicious."

"It's probably nothing," Jessie said. Still, something didn't seem quite right.

As they looked over the titles, Violet remarked, "These books are all about Greek myths."

"What's a myth?" Benny wanted to know.

Jessie smiled at her little brother. "A myth is a kind of story from a long time ago," she explained. "It isn't true. It's just made up."

With their heads bent over their books, the Aldens searched for information about Pandora and her box. Henry came across a story about a winged horse named Pegasus. Then Benny and Violet found one about a girl named Echo, who could only repeat what other people said. Finally, Jessie hit the jackpot.

"I found it!" she said in a loud whisper.

The others leaned closer while Jessie read them the story of Pandora's Box. It was about a girl who received a box on her wedding day. The box came with a warning—it must never be opened. But Pandora, who was a very curious girl, couldn't resist. One day, she opened the lid and peeked inside. All sorts of troubles flew out into the world. When Pandora closed the lid, there was only one thing left inside the box—hope.

As Jessie finished reading, the Aldens looked at each other in bewilderment.

"That was a good story," Benny said. "But how does it fit into the mystery?"

"I can't help wondering about that myself," said Violet. "Any ideas, Henry?"

But Henry didn't answer. His head was bent over another book.

"Henry?" said Jessie. "What are you reading?"

Henry held the book up. "It's called *Fun Facts About Leap Years*," he said. "And guess what? 1904 really *was* a leap year."

"Well, at least that's one thing we're sure about," Violet said, as they pushed back their chairs. "Now if only we could make sense of Pandora's box."

"What do you make of it, Henry?" asked Jessie, as they walked out of the library.

"I think we found another piece of the puzzle," Henry said after a moment's thought. "But I have no idea where it's leading us."

"We'll figure it out," Jessie said, trying to sound positive. "We always do."

Benny rubbed his stomach. "I'm too hungry to think."

"Okay, Benny." Henry laughed. "We'll stop for a bite to eat before we bike out to the Penner place."

It wasn't long before the children had settled into a booth at the Greenfield Diner. A teenaged waitress came over to take their order. She was tall and slim with a heart-shaped face. Her fair hair was pulled back with a headband.

"What will it be?" she said with a friendly smile.

Henry ordered macaroni and cheese and a glass of milk. So did Jessie and Benny.

As the waitress jotted down their orders,

Violet couldn't help thinking she'd seen the waitress somewhere before.

"Violet," Jessie prodded, "do you know what you want?"

But Violet was only half-listening. The more she looked at the waitress, the more certain she was she'd seen her somewhere before. Where was it? Although she was trying not to stare, the waitress caught her look.

"Shall I make it *four* orders of macaroni and cheese?" she questioned Violet.

"Oh!" Violet suddenly snapped out of it. "I'm sorry. I...I was thinking about something."

"Macaroni and cheese?" the waitress asked again.

Violet nodded, then she said, "Don't I know you?"

The waitress giggled a little. "It's funny you should ask me that," she said. "You're the second person to recognize me today."

"Have we met before?" Violet asked.

"No, it's nothing like that." The waitress

leaned forward as if about to share a secret. "I just signed on with the Greenfield Modeling Agency. I've already had a few jobs." She pulled something from her apron pocket and handed it to Violet. It was an ad for Gorman's Drugstore. She pointed to a photograph on the flyer. "That's me holding the bottle of sunscreen lotion."

Benny looked closely at the flyer. "Wow, you're famous!"

The waitress beamed. "You can keep it if you want. I autographed the flyer already. See?" She pointed to a signature—*Carly Boyd*—at the bottom of the ad. "When I become a supermodel, my signature will be worth a fortune!" With that, she dashed away.

"No wonder you recognized her, Violet," said Jessie. "Carly's face is all over town."

Violet frowned. She thought there was more to it than that. But she didn't say anything.

While they waited for their food to arrive, the children talked about the spy game.

"So..." said Jessie. "Pandora closed the box just in time to save hope."

Benny nodded. "Just like Dora."

"What do you mean, Benny?" Henry asked.

"Dora had a box with hope in it, too," Benny explained.

Violet gasped. "Her hope chest!"

"Way to go, Benny!" said Henry. "You're a genius."

The youngest Alden beamed proudly.

"There's only one problem," Jessie pointed out. "We already looked through Dora's hope chest. We didn't find the gold."

"Maybe we missed something," Henry said.

"Like what?" Benny wondered.

Henry grinned. "Like a secret hiding place."

The others thought Henry might be right. They all agreed it was worth checking out.

"One thing we know for sure," said Jessie. "1904 really was a leap year."

"We found out something else, too,"

put in Violet. "Brandon had a sister named Abigail."

"At least, that's what we think," Henry said.

As they were leaving, Violet turned around for one last look at the waitress. She still had the oddest feeling she'd seen her somewhere before—and not on the flyer.

CHAPTER 9

The Plot Thickens

When the Aldens arrived back at the Penner place, they headed straight for the attic. They checked every inch of the hope chest for secret compartments. But they turned up nothing.

"I don't get it," Benny said, the game of checkers tucked under his arm. "I was so sure we were on the right track this time."

Jessie could feel her brother's disappointment. "Never mind," she said, putting a comforting arm around him. "We'll have a nice game of checkers tonight. That'll be fun, right?"

Benny gave a half-hearted smile.

"Do you think we should've checked with Amanda first?" Violet wondered. "Before bringing the game downstairs, I mean."

"I'm sure it'll be fine, Violet," Jessie said as they walked along the hallway.

Once again, the four children paused in front of the photograph of Dora. "There must be a clue we're not seeing," Henry said thoughtfully.

Nobody said anything for a moment. Then Violet suddenly gasped.

"Carly Boyd!" she cried, her eyes wide.

"Are you talking about the waitress at the diner?" Benny asked.

Violet nodded. "I couldn't figure out where I'd seen her before." Seeing their puzzled faces, she added, "Don't you get it? Carly Boyd looks exactly like Dora!"

"What?" Henry laughed. "You're kidding, right?"

Violet pulled the flyer from her back

pocket. "Take a look for yourself," she said, flattening out the creases.

The other Aldens looked from the flyer to the photograph and back again. "I can't believe it!" Jessie said in astonishment.

"Carly looks enough like Dora to be her twin sister," added Henry.

"They have the same heart-shaped faces and fair hair," said Violet, who had an artist's eye for detail.

"And they're both tall and slim," added Jessie. "Carly's the spitting image of Dora, as Grandfather would say."

"It's the strangest thing." Violet felt an icy chill up her spine. "What do you think it means?"

"Maybe Carly's related to the Penner family," Jessie said. "That would explain why they look so much alike."

"We can ask Amanda about it when she gets home," Violet proposed.

Henry had an idea. "Why don't we cool off in the creek while we're waiting?" And the others were quick to agree.

The Aldens changed into their swimsuits, then made their way to Fudge Hollow. They lost all track of time as they splashed around in the creek. The afternoon shadows were growing longer when they finally headed back to the house. After changing back into T-shirts and shorts, they went downstairs to help Mrs. Dawson with dinner. But when they got close to the kitchen, they paused at the sound of Mrs. Dawson's voice.

"No, I'm sure they don't suspect a thing, Steve," Mrs. Dawson was saying. She was talking on the phone, her back to the children. "Yes…I know it would ruin everything if they figure out what's really going on."

The Aldens couldn't believe their ears. Was it possible that Mrs. Dawson and Steve Kooner were partners in crime?

"No, not yet," Mrs. Dawson went on. "But I'm keeping my fingers crossed…If I can open Pandora's box, my dreams will finally come true."

This made Benny gasp, and Mrs. Dawson whirled around. Her eyes widened when she saw the Aldens in the kitchen doorway.

"Oh, you gave me a start!" she cried, hanging up the phone. "I…um, was just…" She didn't seem to know what to say. It was almost as though she'd been caught doing something wrong.

"We thought we'd help with dinner," Violet said quietly.

"Oh, everything's ready, Violet," Mrs. Dawson told her. "I thought chicken and salads would hit the spot. I always say, nothing beats a cold dinner on a hot day." She seemed relieved to be talking about something else.

As the Aldens sat down at the table, Mrs. Dawson hurried out of the room, looking troubled.

"Can you believe it?" Jessie said, keeping her voice low. "Steve and Mrs. Dawson are working together."

"You don't really think they're trying to steal Amanda's gold, do you?" Violet asked.

"I don't want to think that, Violet," Jessie said. "But she was talking about Pandora's box. What else can it mean?"

"It means she's tracking down clues," said Benny.

"And did you notice?" Henry added. "Mrs. Dawson couldn't even look us in the eye."

Violet had to admit it seemed suspicious. But she didn't want to believe Mrs. Dawson would do something so awful.

They were quiet for a while as they ate their dinner. It wasn't until they were clearing the table that Benny spoke up.

"Mrs. Dawson's dream is to open a bookstore," he reminded them. "And that costs a lot of money."

Henry stacked the plates on the counter. "Maybe she'll do whatever it takes to make her dream come true."

"Even stealing from Amanda?" cried Violet.

"We all like her," Jessie told her sister. "But we have to consider every possibility."

Violet opened a drawer. She was looking for a dishtowel. "I know how it sounds, but—" She suddenly stopped talking.

"What's wrong, Violet?" asked Jessie, who

was up to her elbows in soapy water.

"There's something here I think you should see." Violet's eyes were huge. "Something very strange."

The other Aldens hurried over. "I found this under the dishtowels," Violet said, as she removed a photograph from the drawer.

The photo, badly faded with age, showed a dark-haired young woman in a white gown. There was a man in the picture, too. He had a mustache, and his hair was parted in the middle.

Benny had a thought. "I bet that's the missing picture from the family album."

Jessie was staring hard at the photo. "Isn't that Brandon Penner?"

"Got to be," said Henry.

"How can you be so sure?" Benny asked.

"Remember the photo in the family album?" Jessie reminded her little brother. "The one of Brandon Penner, I mean."

"Oh, right!" said Benny. "That does look like the man in the album."

"There's only one problem," Jessie said.

"Who's the woman in this photo?"

"Turn it over," Violet instructed her sister.

Jessie flipped the photograph. She read the words on the back aloud: "The Penners' wedding day—February, 1904."

For a moment, the Aldens just stared at one other in stunned silence. Finally, Henry spoke up.

"How can that be Brandon's wedding day?" he said. "The woman in the wedding dress sure isn't Dora."

"Then...who is she?" Benny asked in a hushed voice.

"It must be Abigail," Violet said as she put the photograph back in the drawer.

Jessie nodded. "Grandfather seemed sure Brandon had married someone named Abigail."

Benny scratched his head. "But...how can there be *two* brides?"

Jessie shrugged. Benny looked at Henry and then at Violet. They didn't seem to have any answers, either.

"If Brandon married Abigail," said Violet, "then who on earth was Dora?"

"I was just wondering the same thing," said Henry. "I can't get my head around it. Can you, Jessie?"

But Jessie didn't answer. She was thinking hard. She had the strangest feeling that she knew something—something important. But it was stuck in the back of her mind and she couldn't shake it loose. Then a funny look suddenly came over her face.

"Don't keep us in the dark, Jessie," Henry pleaded. "What are you thinking?"

"Remember when Amanda dropped a business card the other day?" Jessie said.

Violet nodded. "She tore it up."

"Well, I just remembered something," Jessie continued. "It was a business card for the Greenfield Modeling Agency!"

Henry's eyebrows shot up. "Are you sure, Jessie?"

"Very sure."

"Hey!" said Benny. "Isn't that where Carly Boyd works?"

"Yes, it is," Jessie said with a nod.

"Do you think it's just a coincidence?" asked Violet.

"Maybe," said Jessie. "Or maybe... maybe Carly Boyd doesn't just *look* like Dora Penner—maybe she *is* Dora Penner."

"What do you mean?" Henry asked.

"Listen, Carly looks just like Dora, right? Plus, she's a model for the Greenfield Modeling Agency," said Jessie. "And on top of that, Amanda just happened to have their business card."

"You mean... you think Amanda hired Carly to pose for that photo?" Violet wondered.

"I think it's possible," Jessie replied.

"Amanda tried to fool us?" Benny asked. A frown crossed his round face.

"I can't be sure," said Jessie. "But it looks that way."

"That's interesting Jessie," Henry said. "But why would she do such a thing?"

Before Jessie could answer, they heard the front door open.

"That must be Amanda!" said Violet.

"Let's find out what this is all about," Henry said.

Violet wasn't so sure about this. "But... what if we're wrong?"

"Don't worry, Violet," Henry assured her. "We'll just ask a few questions and see how Amanda reacts. There's nothing wrong with that, is there?"

"No, I suppose not," Violet said.

The Aldens had plenty of questions. The problem was, they didn't have any answers.

CHAPTER 10

A Surprise Twist

"Ah, here you are!" said Amanda, balancing on her crutches. She came into the kitchen with Steve close behind. "I hope Mrs. Dawson fixed you a nice dinner."

"Yes, it was delicious," Violet said.

Amanda looked around at each of the Aldens in turn. "What's up?" she asked, as she sat down at the table. "Everybody looks so serious."

Steve sat down beside Amanda. "Well, detective work is serious business," he said.

"Right, kids?"

Henry squared his shoulders. "Well, it's not just a game to us," he said, looking Steve straight in the eye.

Steve smiled a little. "You kids really don't give up, do you?"

"No, we don't," said Jessie. "Actually, we've been wondering about something."

"Fire away, Jessie," Amanda told her. "Ask me anything."

Jessie hesitated for a moment, then she said, "Was there ever an Abigail in your family?"

"What...?" The question seemed to catch Amanda off guard. But she pulled herself together quickly. "Hmm, let me just think about that." She tapped a finger against her chin thoughtfully. "Now that you mention it," she said at last, "I believe there was an Abigail...somewhere in the family."

"Hard to keep track of everybody, isn't it?" Steve put in, smiling over at Amanda.

"That's for sure!" Amanda said with a nod. "I think there's chocolate cake in the refrigerator," she added, changing the subject.

"Anybody have a sweet tooth?"

But the Aldens weren't going to be put off so easily. "The thing is," Henry said, picking up where Jessie had left off, "Grandfather seemed very sure that Brandon Penner had married somebody named Abigail—not Dora."

"And there's a plaque at the library," added Benny, "with Abigail's name on it."

"Plus, we found a photograph taken on Brandon's wedding day," Violet said in a quiet voice. "The bride didn't look at all like Dora."

Amanda was so startled she needed a few moments to collect her thoughts.

"Well...isn't that strange," she said.

Violet caught a knowing look pass between Amanda and Steve.

"But there can't be two brides," said Benny. "Can there?"

"You wouldn't think so," said Amanda. She forced a laugh as if trying to make light of everything. "If Dora isn't Brandon's bride, I'd sure like to know who she is."

"Carly Boyd," Benny blurted out. "That's who!"

Amanda stared at the youngest Alden in surprise. She opened her mouth to speak, then closed it again. Finally, she let out a sigh. "Oh, dear." She glanced over at Steve. "Things aren't going the way we planned, are they?"

The Aldens looked at each other in surprise. Were Steve and Amanda working together?

"The photograph in the hallway," Henry asked. "Is it really Carly Boyd?"

Amanda nodded. "It is."

"But why?" Jessie said. "Why would you try to fool us?"

"It's not what you think." Amanda said quickly.

Violet's mind raced. Hadn't Steve said something on the phone about a partner in crime—and a plot? And weren't those the very words used to describe the next book in the Detective Club series? Everything suddenly fell into place: Amanda winning awards at school for writing…the set of Detective Club

books tucked away in the dining room...
the way the plot of *The Jigsaw Puzzle Mystery*
sounded familiar.

Jessie looked over at her sister. "Is
something wrong?"

Violet looked from Amanda to Steve and
back again. Then, in a voice scarcely above
a whisper, she said, "You're Mila Jones and
Jake Winston!"

Amanda and Steve looked at each other in
surprise. Then Amanda slowly smiled.

"I guess you found us out," she said.

"Didn't I tell you they were top-notch
detectives?" said Mrs. Dawson, chuckling to
herself as she came into the room.

"Yes, you did." Steve waved a finger at her.
"But you didn't tell us they'd figure out so
much, Mrs. Dawson."

"Is it true?" Jessie asked, her eyes huge.
"Are you really the authors of the Detective
Club books?"

"Yes, we are," said Amanda.

The Aldens looked at one another. For a
moment, they were too amazed to speak.

"I can't believe it!" Henry said at last. "We're sitting with our favorite authors!"

"We've read every book in the Detective Club series!" added Jessie. She sounded just as excited as her older brother.

"I don't get it." Benny looked puzzled. "You mean, you're not really Amanda Penner?"

"Oh, I *am* Amanda Penner, Benny," she assured him. "Mila Jones is my pen name."

"And Jake Winston is *my* pen name," added Steve.

"Sometimes authors use a different name on their books," Henry explained to his younger brother. "It's called a pen name."

"I'm sorry for keeping you in the dark," Amanda said sheepishly. "You see, Steve had his doubts about our latest plot."

"The *Jigsaw Puzzle Mystery*?" guessed Violet.

"Exactly," said Steve, looking surprised that Violet knew that. "I thought some of the clues were too hard for kids to figure out—especially the one about the rings of time."

Amanda added, "When Mrs. Dawson mentioned that you children had solved quite a few mysteries, it got me thinking."

"You decided to test it out," Henry concluded. "The plot, I mean."

Amanda nodded. She explained how they'd needed a photograph of Dora to fit the clues, so they hired Carly Boyd to pose for it. Next, Steve carved the riddle into the stones. The only hitch was finding a good reason for removing the stones from the walkway.

"I twisted my ankle when I was out jogging in Fudge Hollow," Amanda told them. "Why not pretend I tripped over a loose stone in the walkway?"

"I didn't think you kids could solve this mystery," Steve admitted. "But then I saw you at the library today, and I knew you'd figure everything out."

"You were following us, weren't you?" Jessie realized.

"I'm sorry if I frightened you," said Steve. "I just happened to be passing by and I saw you go inside. I was curious to see how you were making out with the mystery. When I saw you browsing through books on Greek myths, I knew you were doing just fine." Then he turned to Mrs. Dawson. "You were right about these kids," he said. "They don't miss a thing."

"So you were in on this, too, Mrs. Dawson?" asked Jessie.

"Yes, that's why I went out to your house the other day," Mrs. Dawson confessed. "I knew if I mentioned the loose stones, you would offer to help."

"Grandfather thought it was a coincidence," said Henry, "that the kids you hired happened to be detectives."

Jessie had a sudden thought. "When you were visiting with Mrs. McGregor the other day, you spilled the cream on purpose, didn't you, Mrs. Dawson?"

"Yes, I did," said Mrs. Dawson. "I didn't want to talk about Amanda's writing, so…"

"You tried to distract everyone," finished Henry.

Mrs. Dawson nodded. "I knew what good

detectives you were. I was afraid you'd have everything figured out in no time if I said too much."

Benny looked confused. "There's one thing I don't understand, Mrs. Dawson," he said. "If you were in on everything, why were you tracking down clues?"

"*Me?*" Mrs. Dawson pointed to herself. Then she began to laugh. "Why would you think I was tracking down clues?"

"You said if you opened Pandora's box," Benny told her, "then all your dreams would come true."

"Oh, you heard that, did you?" said Mrs. Dawson. Then she turned to Steve. "That must have been when you phoned."

"Neither Amanda nor I could stand the suspense," Steve said with a laugh. "We just had to find out if the bank had approved Mrs. Dawson's business loan."

"Well, guess what?" Mrs. Dawson's face broke into a big smile. "The bank manager just called and gave me the thumbs up! Looks like my dream really will come true."

Turning to the youngest Alden, she added, "When you heard me on the phone, Benny, I was talking about opening my bookstore. You see, I decided to call it Pandora's Box."

"Oh!" The children looked at each other in sudden understanding.

As everyone congratulated Mrs. Dawson, Henry noticed the game of checkers on top of the refrigerator. He suddenly thought of something. In a flash, he was on his feet. Reaching the box of checkers down, he came back to the table.

Jessie could tell by the look on her older brother's face that something was up. "What's going on, Henry?"

"We missed something," Henry said. "There was a clue in the first riddle, but we didn't pick up on it."

"What?" asked Benny.

Curious, Jessie tugged her notebook from her pocket. After flipping through the pages, she recited, *"Follow the clues/ both night and day;/ leave no stone unturned/ the game's in play."*

Violet slapped a hand against her forehead. "Oh, the *game's in play!*"

"The game of checkers," Jessie realized. "How could we miss that?"

"Open it, Henry!" Benny inched his chair closer.

As Henry lifted the lid from the box of checkers, Amanda and Steve seemed to be holding their breath. Even Mrs. Dawson was standing as still as a statue.

Inside the box, they found a folded checker board and a cloth bag. Henry gave the bag a shake, but there weren't many checkers inside.

"That's odd," said Jessie.

Henry held the bag upside down and gave it a shake. When Amanda caught a glimpse of what tumbled out, her jaw dropped.

"What in the world...?" she cried out in astonishment.

"Oooh!" cried Violet. "It's a diamond ring."

Sure enough, a sparkling diamond on a gold band came to rest in the middle of the

checker board. It was clear Amanda couldn't quite believe what she was seeing.

"But we put chocolate coins in that bag—wrapped in gold foil," she said in bewilderment. "Do you know anything about this, Steve?"

Jessie couldn't help noticing that beads of perspiration had popped up on Steve's forehead. He was mopping at his face with a handkerchief.

"Steve?" Amanda repeated.

To everyone's astonishment, Steve suddenly knelt down on one knee beside Amanda's chair. Reaching for her hand, he said, "Will you marry me?"

For a long moment, Amanda stared at Steve. Then her face broke into a smile. "Of course, I'll marry you!"

The Aldens let out a cheer as Steve slipped the engagement ring onto Amanda's finger.

"Oh, how romantic!" gushed Mrs. Dawson, wiping away a tear of joy.

"You planned this all along, didn't you, Steve?" Amanda said, admiring her ring.

Beaming happily, Steve got to his feet. "I wanted to propose in a special way," he said. "I thought—what would be better than to make it part of a mystery."

Violet smiled to herself. Steve hadn't been looking for the "rings of time"—he was looking for an engagement ring for Amanda!

Benny had a question. "Did your grandfather really play the spy game with you, Amanda?" he wanted to know. "Or did you make that part up, too?"

"Oh, that was true, Benny," Amanda assured him. "In fact, that's how I got the idea for *The Jigsaw Puzzle Mystery*. It's because of my grandfather," she added, "that I love mysteries so much."

Jessie was wondering about something, too. "The day you surprised us with that picnic lunch," she said, "you were trying to give us a hint, weren't you, Amanda?"

Amanda didn't deny it. "I wanted to point you towards Fudge Hollow."

"You gave us another hint, too," Violet realized, "when you said there might be family photos in the hope chest."

"Right again," said Amanda.

This made Mrs. Dawson laugh. "I don't think these children needed any hints," she said. "They figured everything out—and more!"

Steve was quick to agree. "The kids in the Detective Club books couldn't have done it better. And thanks to the Aldens," he added, "we can send *The Jigsaw Puzzle Mystery* off to the publishers."

"I can't wait till it comes out!" said Benny.

Amanda looked over at Steve. With a quick nod, Steve hurried out of the room. He came back a moment later holding a stack of typed pages tied together with string.

"You won't have to wait, Benny," Steve said, placing the bundle on the table. "We made an extra copy of *The Jigsaw Puzzle Mystery*."

"You mean, we can read it?" Benny asked in disbelief.

"Before it's even published?" added Jessie.

"You sure can," said Amanda. "But first,

it needs a dedication." Fishing a pen from her purse, she wrote something on the first page. Then she passed the manuscript to the Aldens.

When Jessie took a closer look, her eyes widened and she gasped.

"What is it?" asked Benny. "What does it say?"

Jessie read the dedication aloud:

To Henry, Violet, Benny, and Jessie, the world's greatest detectives!

"Yippee!" cried Benny. "We'll be famous."

"I think this calls for a celebration," said Mrs. Dawson, as everyone laughed. "Anybody for chocolate cake?"

Benny raised his hand high in the air. "My two favorite things," he said with a grin. "Food *and* a mystery!"